chloe willette 2007

thet I wrote
chloe willetter

© 1994 Grandreams Limited.

Published by
Grandreams Limited
Jadwin House, 205/211 Kentish Town Road, London,
NW5 2JU.

Printed in Italy.
BW5-8

Gulliver's Travels

Illustrated by Pam Storey.
Stories re-told by Grace De La Touche.

I accepted an offer to be surgeon on board the *Antelope*, which was sailing to the South Seas. The ship left Bristol on 4th May, 1699.

The early stages of our voyage were very prosperous, but when we were north of Van Diemen's land, a violent storm blew us far off course. On 5th November, we were blown onto a rock, and the ship broke up! We were thrown overboard!

I swam and floated for as long as I could, but saw no-one from the ship. I often

let my legs drop to see if I could touch bottom, but there was nothing to feel. Eventually when I thought I was near the end, I again let my legs drop - and this time there was land beneath my feet!

I walked and walked, and the land gradually sloped up, and after about a mile I reached a beach. I walked another half a mile, but saw no sign of life. Finally, I collapsed, and being so weary fell into a deep sleep. It was near daylight when I woke up. I tried to rise, but I could not!

"What's this?" I cried. I

was lying on my back, and realised that my arms and legs were tied down. My hair, being quite long, was also tied down. Several fine ropes passed over my body, binding me to the ground. All I could do was look straight up. The sun grew hotter and brighter. I could hear noises around me, but could only look up.

Suddenly I felt something alive moving on my left leg! It advanced up my body, and on to my chest. I looked down at it, as well as I could without moving my head. It stood just by my chin, and I saw it was a small human creature! It was no more than six inches high, holding a bow and arrow, with a quiver on its back. At the same time, I felt about forty more of the same creatures following the first.

"Aah!" I yelled out, in a loud voice.

They all ran back in fright, and I was told later that some hurt themselves in their haste to jump off me. However, they soon returned, and one ventured close enough to look at my face.

"Hekinah Degul!" the little figure cried out in a shrill

voice. The others repeated these words, which at this time meant nothing to me.

As you will no doubt understand I felt very uneasy, tied down to the ground. I moved slowly, and managed to free my left arm. I felt my head, and worked out how I was held down. A painful pull, and I found I could move my head a couple of inches.

The creatures ran off before I could seize them, and this time there was a great cry of, "Tolgo Phonac!"

An instant later, I felt a hundred pinpricks in my left

hand as the little people let go a flight of their arrows. They immediately released another flight, and some hit my face. I groaned with the pain, and tried to loosen the bonds, but only received another volley of arrows for my trouble. Some even tried to stab me with spears!

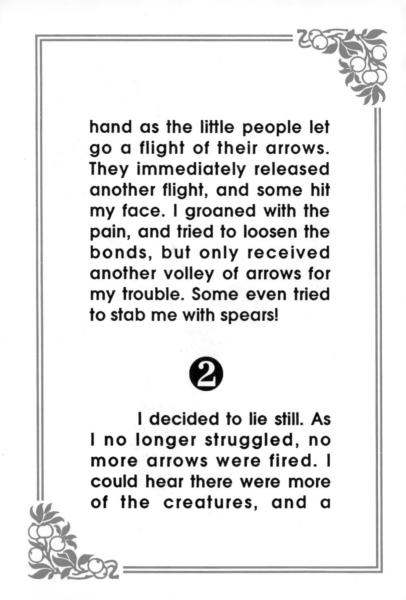

2

I decided to lie still. As I no longer struggled, no more arrows were fired. I could hear there were more of the creatures, and a

knocking of wood told me they were building something.

When I strained my head to the right I saw a stage, about a foot and a half high. They released my hair on the left so that I might look to the right, and hear the speech.

"Langro Dehul san!" the little person cried out three times, before starting his speech. I didn't understand a word he said, but I could tell from his manner when he was threatening, or promising things or being kind. I'm

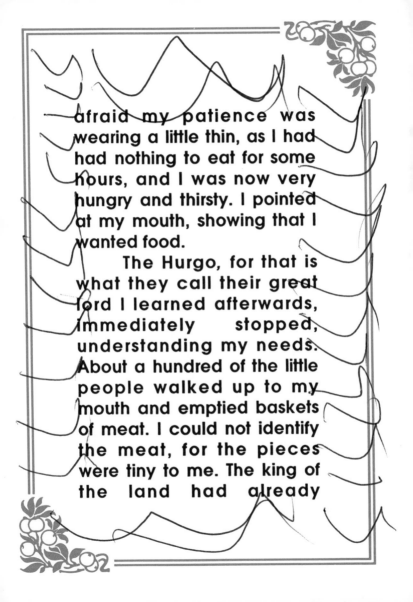

afraid my patience was wearing a little thin, as I had had nothing to eat for some hours, and I was now very hungry and thirsty. I pointed at my mouth, showing that I wanted food.

The Hurgo, for that is what they call their great lord I learned afterwards, immediately stopped, understanding my needs. About a hundred of the little people walked up to my mouth and emptied baskets of meat. I could not identify the meat, for the pieces were tiny to me. The king of the land had already anticipated my needs, and had ordered the meat to be collected as soon as he had heard of my capture. I was able to eat two or three baskets full at a time, and the people gasped at my appetite.

The same method was used to give me a drink. This time they hauled up two giant hogsheads of wine, which contained about half a pint each.

The people danced on my chest, and I was half-tempted to pull myself up and catch a good handful, but I felt the arrows were not

the worst they could throw at me, and they had fed me, so I decided to wait.

A while later, a representative of the king made his way up my body, and stopped at my chin. He showed me a stamped document, his credentials, and then spoke for ten minutes. He kept pointing inland, to where the capital city lay about half a mile away. The king had ordered that I be taken there.

I gestured to my bonds, asking that I might be freed.

"No," came back the reply, in their own language. I would be transported there, and I should have no worry about food or drink, I would be well treated.

I again struggled to free myself, but a shower of arrows at my face and hands stopped me. I therefore made it understood that they could do as they wished. The Hurgo and his people were happy with this. I was released on one side, and I went to sleep again. A sleeping potion had been added to the wine.

I was afterwards told that as soon as news of my arrival had reached the capital city, the king and his council had given orders that I be tied down, that food and wine be collected, and that a great machine be built to carry me to the city.

The people were great mathematicians, and had already built machines for carrying great trees, or for carrying ships from the wood to the sea. The king therefore ordered that the biggest one yet should be built. It set out four hours after my landing. The main difficulty was placing me on the frame. Eighty poles were erected, and by ropes and pulleys, nine hundred of the strongest men pulled me on to the engine. All this was done while I lay in my drugged sleep. Fifteen hundred of the king's horses pulled the engine to the capital. We arrived the next day.

The king and his court came to welcome us. We had stopped by an old temple, the largest in the kingdom. This would be my

new lodgings. The temple door was some four foot high, and so I could enter easily and lay down at full length inside. A chain was fastened to my ankle, and when the guards were sure I could not escape, the ties were released.

4

Imagine the surprise of the people when I stood and walked. I looked about me, and could see the square fields spreading out like flower beds. The tallest trees

were no more than seven feet high.

The king rode up with his attendants to look at me. Food and drink again arrived, which I quickly ate and drank. I then lay on the ground, so that my face was about three yards away from the king's. I have since held him in my hand, but at that moment, I was speaking in every language I knew to make myself understood. But it was to no purpose, and after two hours the king and his court retired.

The guard continued to protect me from a crowd.

Arrows were fired at me as I sat by my door, and six ringleaders were rounded up and pushed towards me for punishment. I tucked five of them in my pocket, and held onto the sixth. I made as if to put him in my mouth. The poor man screamed, and the guards pulled a pained face. Instead I pulled out a penknife and cut his bonds and put him gently on his feet. I took the rest from my pocket, one at a time, and did the same. Report of this was soon given to the king and council.

When night came, I lay

on the stony ground of the temple floor. But within a fortnight a huge bed had been made for me, and also covers and blankets. News of my arrival spread through the kingdom, and people came from far and wide to look at me.

Meanwhile, the king and council were having many meetings to discuss my arrival. Food was a great problem, and they feared I would cause a famine. It was suggested that I be shot with poisonous arrows, but they didn't like the thought of a great carcass rotting so

close to the city, which might cause disease.

News of my actions towards the six men was reported in the midst of these meetings, and the king gave orders that food be provided, that servants be on hand for me, that a suit be made for me and that six of the country's best teachers teach me their language.

Within three weeks, I had made great progress, and the king would come nearly every day to help the teachers. As soon as I was able, I asked him at every visit for my freedom. I

understood from his answer that I would have to swear a peace with him and his kingdom. He advised me to be patient.

I was gentle and well-behaved with the little people, and soon had hopes of being freed. I was learning the language, and the people were becoming brave enough to come and see me and for the children to even play in my hair.

Eventually I was granted my freedom. My behaviour had pleased the king and his council. Only one councillor objected, Skyresh Bolgolam, who for some unknown reason became my mortal enemy.

The king was there when the chain was struck, and I lay down at his feet. He told me to arise, saying that he hoped I would be a good and faithful servant.

My first request was to see the capital city, and my wish was granted. Orders were given for all the people to keep in their houses. I stepped over the wall into the city. The two wide main streets cut the town into four. The houses were from three to five storeys high, and seemed to be full of people, for the city could hold five hundred thousand souls.

The palace was in the centre, where the two main streets met, but unfortunately I could not enter the main courtyard as the buildings of the inner court were over five foot high.

A second visit was arranged, and in the meantime, I made myself two stools to bridge the

buildings and was thus able to see into the richly decorated royal apartments, and to see the queen and the royal family.

Two weeks or so later, I had a visit from Reldresal the principal secretary, who wished to speak with me privately.

"You will know that the court is divided into two factions, the High Heels and the Low Heels. The king favours the Low Heels in the administration, whereas the crown prince seems to favour the High Heels, as one of his heels is higher than the other.

In the midst of this, we are threatened with an invasion from the island of Blefuscu, which is almost as big as this empire. We have heard you talk about your people, and your kingdoms, but our philosophers are inclined to believe that you fell from the sky. For in all our long history, we know only of two kingdoms, Lilliput and Blefuscu. We have been at war for some time. It came about when the present king's grandfather, when breaking the egg in the time-honoured way at the larger end, happened to cut

his finger. His father immediately announced that eggs should be broken at the smaller end by all his subjects, with severe penalties for those not obeying. The people did not like this law and there have since been six rebellions. One king has lost his life, another his throne.

"Those who disagreed have fled to Blefuscu, where their king protects them. Now they are preparing a great fleet to sail against us. The king has told me to put all this before you."

"I cannot interfere with

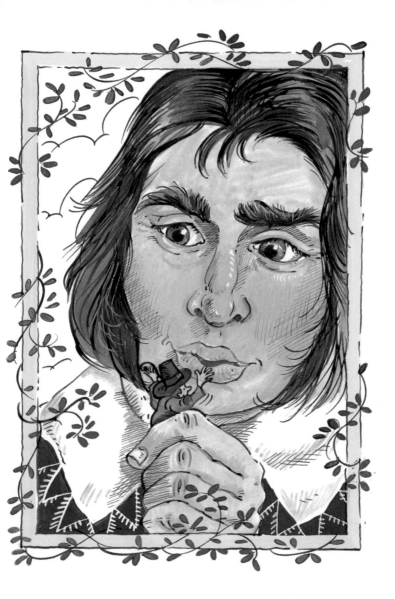

your beliefs and politics," I said politely. "But I will do all I can to protect the king and his country."

Blefuscu lay about eight hundred yards off the north east coast of Lilliput. At its deepest, the channel was about six foot deep. I walked to the north east, and lying behind a hillock, viewed the opposing navy with my eyeglass. It was at rest in a bay. There were about fifty Men of War, and many

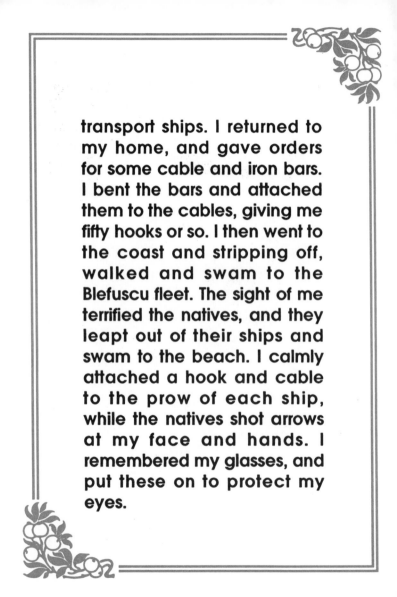

transport ships. I returned to my home, and gave orders for some cable and iron bars. I bent the bars and attached them to the cables, giving me fifty hooks or so. I then went to the coast and stripping off, walked and swam to the Blefuscu fleet. The sight of me terrified the natives, and they leapt out of their ships and swam to the beach. I calmly attached a hook and cable to the prow of each ship, while the natives shot arrows at my face and hands. I remembered my glasses, and put these on to protect my eyes.

The Blefuscudians did not know what I was up to, until I began to pull the ships away behind me. They then began to scream and cry out, and continued to fire their arrows.

The king and his whole court stood on the shore, and could see the ships moving towards them, but initially could not see me and so feared that the whole mission had gone wrong and that the fleet was now attacking. But as I passed through to the shallow part I could be seen and the cheering began. The king was so delighted he made me a Nardac on the spot, which is a very high honour.

The king immediately ordered me to return and bring the remaining ships, so that he could eventually make the island into a province of Lilliput, and be the one king. But I protested, saying that I would not be used to bring a free people into slavery. It turned out that most of the council agreed with me, but the king never forgave me for upsetting a great royal plan, even though I had done him a great service.

Three weeks later an envoy arrived from Blefuscu with offers of peace. These were very advantageous to our king. I met with the envoys and begged them to give my best wishes to their emperor, and that I would try to visit his court before I returned to my own country.

On my next meeting with the king, I asked permission to meet the Blefuscudian emperor, and this was very coldly given. I was beginning to have some inkling of how the court and ministers thought.

7

While I was preparing for my visit to Blefuscu, I had a visitor from court. He came secretly, wanting to save my honour and my life, as I had once done his.

"You know that Bolgolam hates you, especially since your success with the Blefuscudian navy. Well, he and the High Treasurer have prepared a document against you, accusing you of treason and other crimes," he told me. "For disobeying the king when he ordered you to go back and take the rest of the ships, for talking with the Blefuscudian envoy when they had so recently been an enemy of the king, and for now preparing to go to the Blefuscudian court, to offer help and comfort."

I was amazed.

"The king did speak up for you, but the Admiral and Treasurer want you to die as painful a death as possible. But the king was determined to spare your life and he asked Reldresal his opinion. Reldresal said

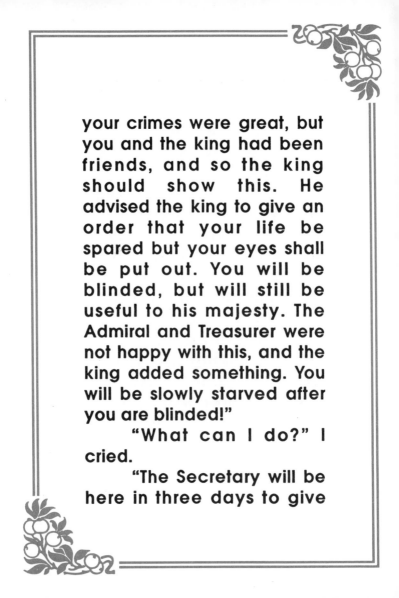

your crimes were great, but
you and the king had been
friends, and so the king
should show this. He
advised the king to give an
order that your life be
spared but your eyes shall
be put out. You will be
blinded, but will still be
useful to his majesty. The
Admiral and Treasurer were
not happy with this, and the
king added something. You
will be slowly starved after
you are blinded!"

"What can I do?" I
cried.

"The Secretary will be
here in three days to give

you the sentence, but it is your decision what you do," said my visitor. "I must go."

I sat alone, puzzled and astonished. I did not wait long. I sent a letter to the secretary, telling him of my intention to visit the Blefuscudian court, as I had been given permission to do, and without waiting for a reply, set out. I put my clothes in a man of war, and towed it to the harbour at Blefuscu.

The people were waiting for me, and showed me to the capital city. The prince made me very welcome.

8

Three days later, I was on the north coast, and I saw what looked like a boat. I waded out and saw that it was a real boat, possibly blown in by a storm. The tide was driving it closer in, and after great effort I was able to bring it into shore, and saw that it was not badly damaged. I had oars to make, and then I had a boat that could take me back to my own country.

I wondered that I had not heard anything from

Lilliput, but I learned that the king was not initially suspicious of my absence. But when several days had elapsed, he sent an envoy telling the prince to return me bound, hand and foot, to receive punishment.

The prince consulted for three days, and then sent the envoy back saying he could not send me back, and anyway, the problem would soon be solved as I had found a boat to take me away from the islands.

The prince told me this, and offered his protection should I wish to stay. I declined, and prepared for my departure. A month later, sails and ropes were made, and the little boat was loaded with food, and I took some live cows and sheep with me to breed.

I set out early one morning, sailing north, and after just two days of sailing I saw a sail. It was a ship, and English at that! I even met an old friend on board, who thought I was raving when I told him of my adventures until I showed him the live cows and sheep!

Happily we arrived back in England safely and prosperously.